DATE DUE

Jr. Graphic Mysteries™

ATLANTIS

The Mystery of the Lost City

Jack DeMolay

PowerKiDS press™

New York

Published in 2007 by the Rosen Publishing Group, Inc.
29 East 21st Street, New York, NY 10010

First Edition

Editor: Joanne Randolph
Book Design: Ginny Chu
Illustrations: Q2A

Library of Congress Cataloging-in-Publication Data

DeMolay, Jack.
  Atlantis : the mystery of the lost city / by Jack DeMolay.— 1st ed.
      p. cm. — (Jr. graphic mysteries)
  Includes index.
  ISBN (10) 1-4042-3407-1 — (13) 978-1-4042-3407-9 (library binding) — ISBN
(10) 1-4042-2160-3 — (13) 978-1-4042-2160-4 (pbk)
  1. Atlantis—Juvenile literature. I. Title. II. Series.
GN751.D384 2007
398.23'4—dc22
                                      2006003854

Manufactured in the United States of America

Contents

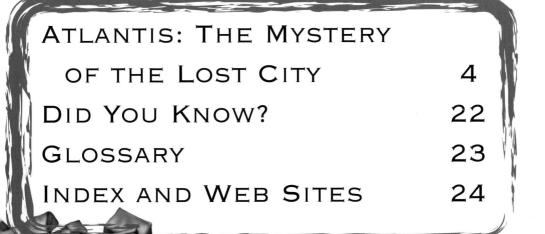

ATLANTIS:
THE MYSTERY OF THE LOST CITY

HAVE YOU EVER HEARD THE **LEGEND** OF THE ANCIENT CITY OF ATLANTIS? IS THE STORY TRUE? WAS IT TRULY ONE OF THE GREATEST CITIES ON EARTH AT ONE TIME?

HOW DID IT FALL TO THE BOTTOM OF THE SEA? MOST IMPORTANT OF ALL, WHERE EXACTLY MIGHT THIS LOST CITY BE LOCATED?

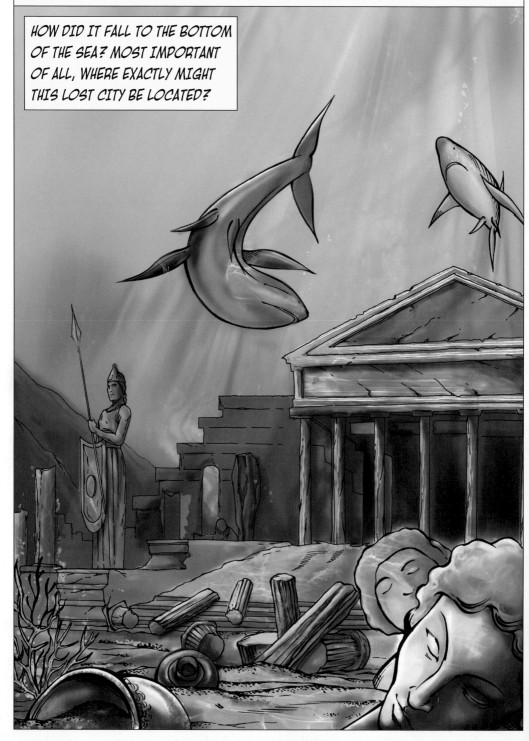

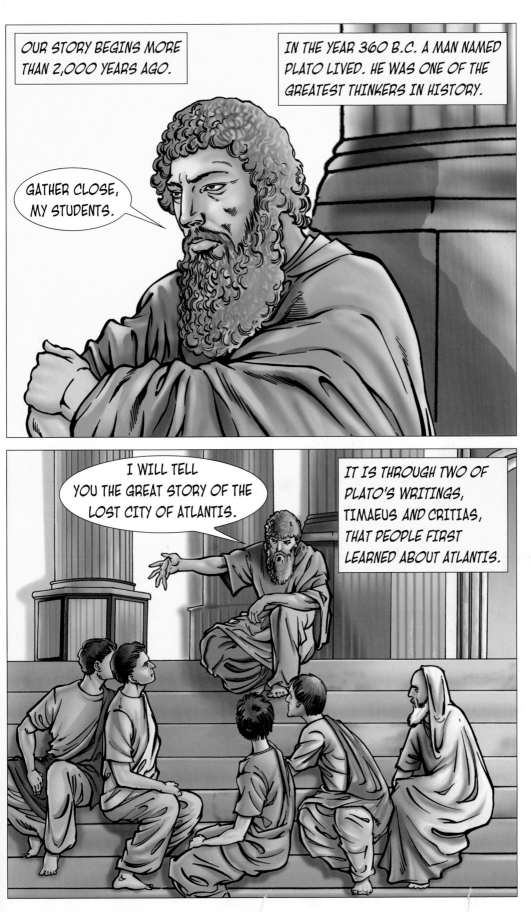

PLATO DESCRIBED ATLANTIS AS AN ANCIENT
SOCIETY WITH ADVANCED **TECHNOLOGY**.

TO UNDERSTAND HOW AND WHY ATLANTIS SANK TO THE BOTTOM OF THE SEA, IT IS
IMPORTANT TO KNOW MORE ABOUT THIS CITY.

PLATO DESCRIBED ATLANTIS AS HAVING THE MOST TALENTED BUILDERS EVER. THEY BUILT BEAUTIFUL TEMPLES, PALACES, AND OTHER BUILDINGS.

THEY ALSO CONSTRUCTED A **COMPLICATED** SYSTEM OF WATERWAYS, WHICH INCLUDED HARBORS AND DOCKS.

THEY BUILT FOUNTAINS THAT RAN BOTH COLD AND HOT WATER.

ALL THIS HIGHLY ADVANCED BUILDING TOOK PLACE MORE THAN 12,000 YEARS AGO.

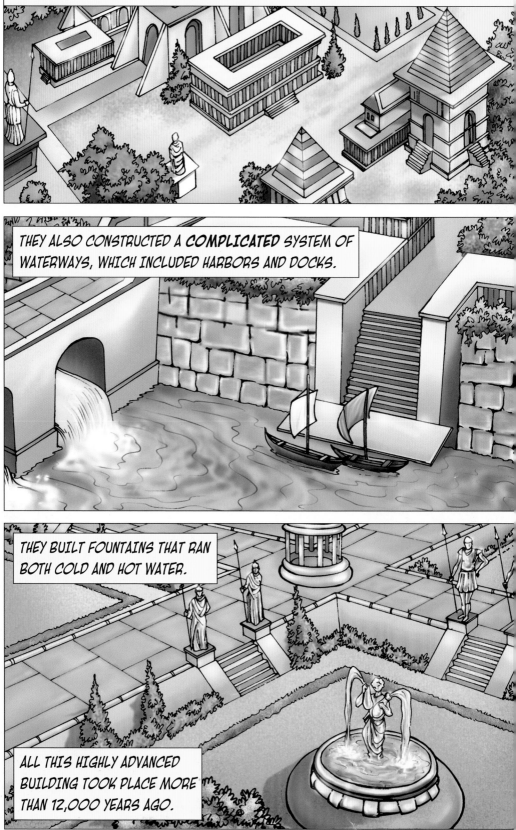

POSEIDON AND HIS WIFE HAD 10 SONS. AFTER THEY GREW UP, EACH SON RULED A DIFFERENT PART OF HIS PARENTS' GREAT KINGDOM.

FOR MANY YEARS, ATLANTIS WAS RULED PEACEFULLY.

POSEIDON'S SONS SOON BEGAN TO FIGHT. EACH THOUGHT HIS BROTHERS HAD A BETTER PIECE OF THE KINGDOM. EACH SON WANTED MORE LAND.

THIS KINGDOM SHALL BE MINE!

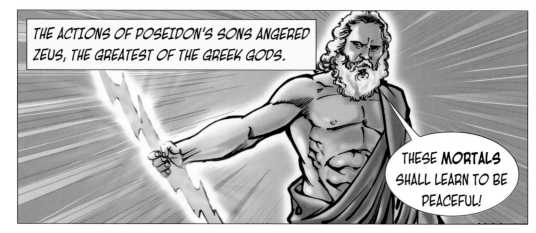

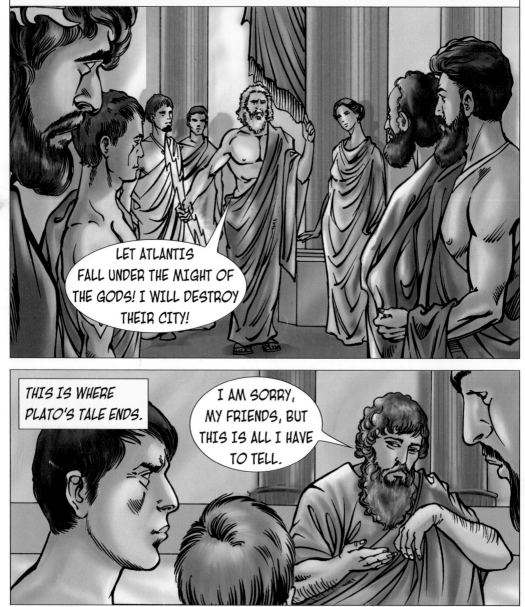

FOR CENTURIES, **SCHOLARS** HAVE GUESSED WHAT MIGHT HAVE HAPPENED TO ATLANTIS. THERE ARE TWO THINGS ON WHICH ALMOST ALL THE SCHOLARS AGREE.

ATLANTIS WAS OVERCOME BY HUGE OCEAN WAVES AND DESTROYED.

MOST SCHOLARS ALSO AGREE THAT ABSOLUTELY NO ONE LIVED.

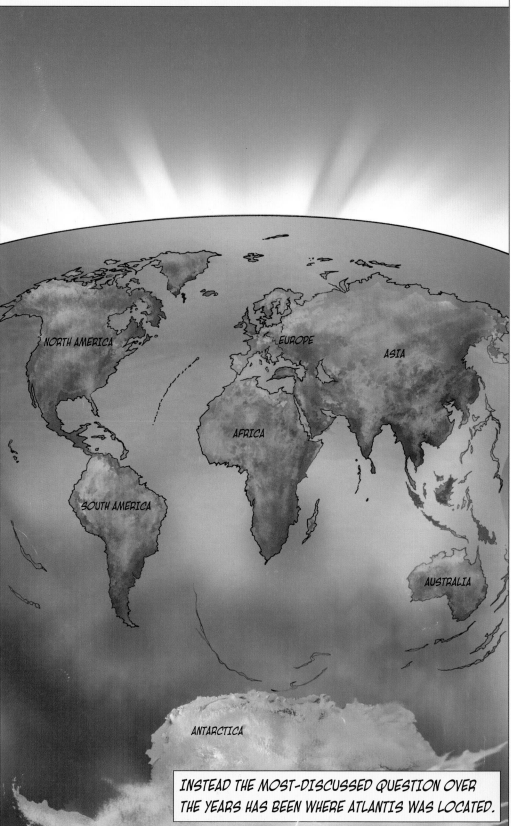

THE MOST MYSTERIOUS QUESTION OF ALL IS NOT HOW ATLANTIS WAS DESTROYED, THOUGH. IT IS NOT EVEN WHETHER ATLANTIS ACTUALLY EXISTED.

INSTEAD THE MOST-DISCUSSED QUESTION OVER THE YEARS HAS BEEN WHERE ATLANTIS WAS LOCATED.

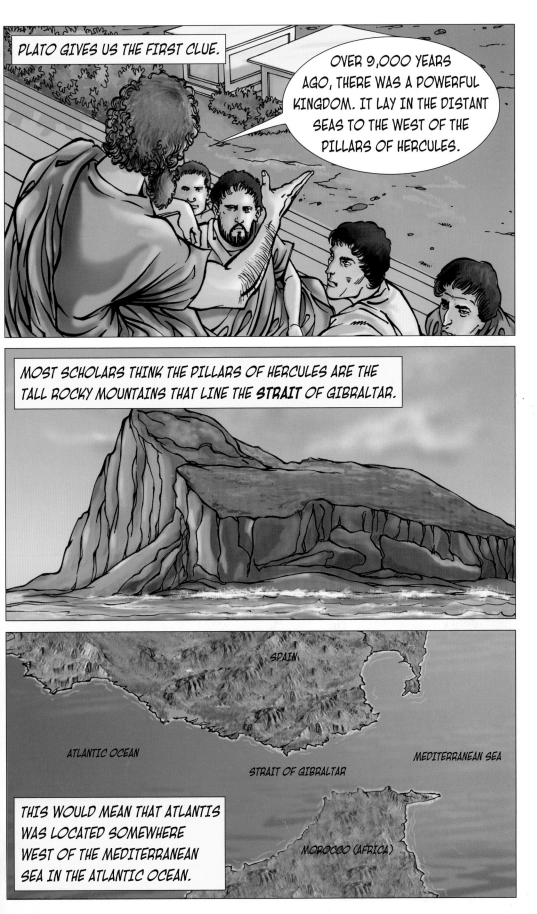

PLATO GIVES US THE FIRST CLUE.

OVER 9,000 YEARS AGO, THERE WAS A POWERFUL KINGDOM. IT LAY IN THE DISTANT SEAS TO THE WEST OF THE PILLARS OF HERCULES.

MOST SCHOLARS THINK THE PILLARS OF HERCULES ARE THE TALL ROCKY MOUNTAINS THAT LINE THE **STRAIT** OF GIBRALTAR.

SPAIN

ATLANTIC OCEAN

STRAIT OF GIBRALTAR

MEDITERRANEAN SEA

MOROCCO (AFRICA)

THIS WOULD MEAN THAT ATLANTIS WAS LOCATED SOMEWHERE WEST OF THE MEDITERRANEAN SEA IN THE ATLANTIC OCEAN.

MANY SCHOLARS THINK THE AZORES ISLANDS ARE THE REMAINS OF THE LOST KINGDOM OF ATLANTIS.

THEY BELIEVE THAT THE ISLANDS ARE ACTUALLY THE TOPS OF MOUNTAINS ON ATLANTIS, WHICH ARE NOW UNDER THE SEA.

HOWEVER, **SURVEYS** OF THE OCEAN FLOOR AROUND THIS AREA SHOW NO SIGN OF ANY UNDERWATER BUILDINGS.

OTHER SCIENTISTS THINK THAT ATLANTIS MIGHT LIE TO THE EAST OF THE PILLARS OF HERCULES RATHER THAN THE WEST.

THEY ALSO THINK THAT ATLANTIS MAY HAVE BEEN LOST 900 YEARS BEFORE THE TIME OF PLATO, INSTEAD OF 9,000 YEARS.

THESE SCIENTISTS THINK THAT ATLANTIS MIGHT HAVE BEEN THE ISLAND OF CRETE.

IN MODERN TIMES, CRETE BELONGS TO THE NATION OF GREECE.

IT IS LOCATED SOUTH OF THE GREEK MAINLAND IN THE MIDDLE OF THE MEDITERRANEAN SEA.

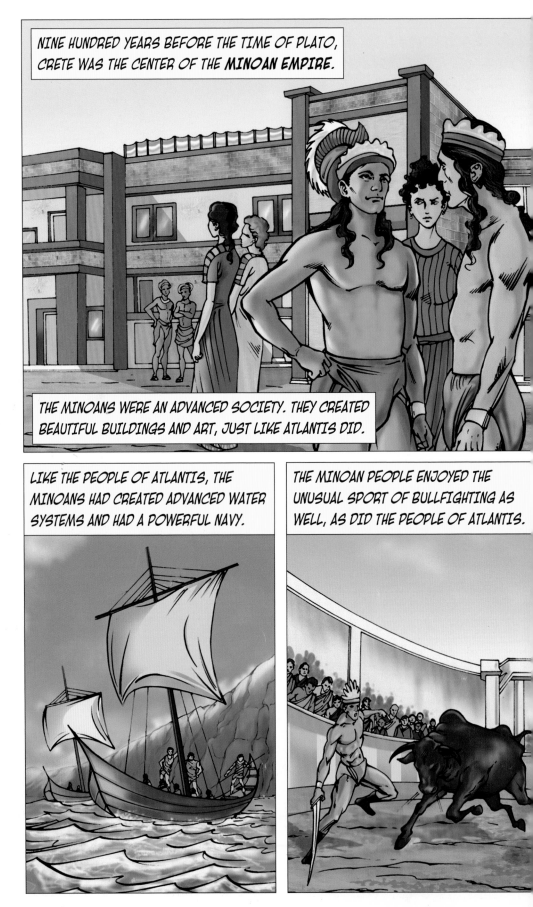

NINE HUNDRED YEARS BEFORE THE TIME OF PLATO, CRETE WAS THE CENTER OF THE **MINOAN EMPIRE.**

THE MINOANS WERE AN ADVANCED SOCIETY. THEY CREATED BEAUTIFUL BUILDINGS AND ART, JUST LIKE ATLANTIS DID.

LIKE THE PEOPLE OF ATLANTIS, THE MINOANS HAD CREATED ADVANCED WATER SYSTEMS AND HAD A POWERFUL NAVY.

THE MINOAN PEOPLE ENJOYED THE UNUSUAL SPORT OF BULLFIGHTING AS WELL, AS DID THE PEOPLE OF ATLANTIS.

MOST SCIENTISTS SAY THAT THE MINOAN WAY OF LIFE ENDED WITH A **VOLCANIC ERUPTION** NEAR THE ISLAND OF SANTORINI.

THIS ERUPTION IS THOUGHT TO HAVE BEEN ONE OF THE MOST POWERFUL IN EARTH'S HISTORY.

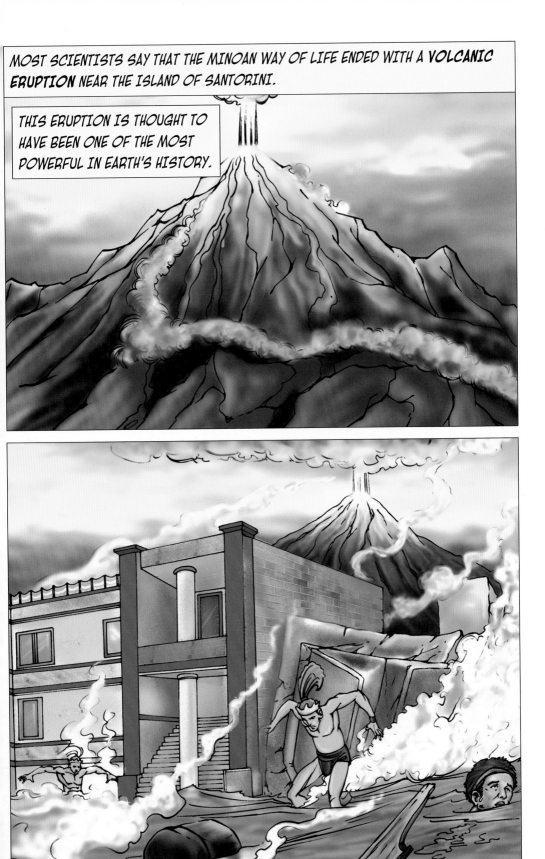

THE VOLCANO WOULD HAVE CREATED A LARGE TIDAL WAVE. SCIENTISTS THINK THIS WAVE MAY HAVE DESTROYED EVERYTHING ON CRETE AND KILLED THE MINOAN PEOPLE.

COULD CRETE AND ATLANTIS BE ONE AND THE SAME? IF PLATO MADE A MISTAKE, THEN THERE IS A STRONG CHANCE THIS COULD BE TRUE.

WHAT IF PLATO WAS NOT WRONG, THOUGH?

THE LIST OF POSSIBLE LOCATIONS FOR ATLANTIS GROWS WITH EACH PASSING YEAR.

THIS ANCIENT CITY COULD HAVE EXISTED WHERE MODERN-DAY SPAIN, BERMUDA, NEW ZEALAND, PERU, TURKEY, OR CUBA ARE LOCATED.

CUBA SEEMS TO BE THE LOCATION MANY SCHOLARS AGREE ON TODAY.

WHAT APPEAR TO BE MANMADE BUILDINGS HAVE BEEN DISCOVERED UNDERWATER OFF THE COAST OF CUBA.

CUBA'S GOVERNMENT HAS NOT YET GIVEN PERMISSION TO VISIT AND STUDY THESE UNDERWATER BUILDINGS.

THIS MEANS MANY QUESTIONS REMAIN UNANSWERED.

NO MATTER WHERE ATLANTIS IS LOCATED, IT WILL ALWAYS REMAIN A POPULAR SUBJECT OF DISCUSSION.

STORIES ABOUT THIS MYSTERIOUS CITY WILL FOREVER LINE THE **SHELVES** OF BOOKSTORES.

THIS PERFECT CITY THAT HAS BEEN LOST BENEATH THE OCEAN WILL FOREVER CAPTURE OUR IMAGINATIONS.

IS PROOF OF ATLANTIS AT THE BOTTOM OF THE SEA SOMEWHERE, JUST WAITING TO BE DISCOVERED?

UNTIL THAT DAY, THE SEARCH FOR THE TRUTH BEHIND THIS LOST CITY WILL CONTINUE.

THE END

Did You Know?

- According to Plato's writings, the farmers of Atlantis grew their food on a field a little larger than the state of Oklahoma.

- The Greek word *Atlantis* means "island of Atlas." Atlas was the oldest son of Poseidon and his wife.

- Atlantis scholar Edgar Cayce believed that Atlantis had aircraft and ships powered by a mysterious crystal.

- Edgar Cayce was also known as the sleeping prophet, because many of his ideas about Atlantis came to him in dreams.

- J.R.R. Tolkien included elements of the Atlantis story in his book *The Silmarillion*.

Glossary

complicated (KOM-pluh-kayt-ed) Hard to understand.

legend (LEH-jend) A story, passed down through the years, that cannot be proved.

Minoan Empire (meh-NOH-en EM-pyr) A society in Crete in the Aegean Sea that lived from 3000 B.C. to 1450 B.C.

mortals (MOR-tulz) Human beings.

punish (PUH-nish) To cause someone pain or loss for a crime he or she has committed.

scholars (SKAH-lerz) People who have gone to school and who have much knowledge.

strait (STRAYT) A narrow waterway connecting two larger bodies of water.

surveys (SER-vayz) Studies of the land.

technology (tek-NAH-luh-jee) The way that people do something using tools and the tools that they use.

volcanic eruption (vol-KA-nik ih-RUP-shun) When magma comes through an opening in Earth's crust.

Index

Web Sites

Due to the changing nature of Internet links, the Rosen Publishing Group, Inc., has developed an online list of Web sites related to the subject of this book. This site is updated regularly. Please use this link to access the list:
www.powerkidslinks.com/jgm/atlantis/